Chief Inspector Albert Stagnetto, 52 years old, twenty-two years with Gibraltar Constabulary. Born to a Maltese father and a Spanish mother. Prior to the police, served ten years in the British Army.

Married to Carmen Lopez, now a naturalised Gibraltarian, and her parents are Spanish, both from old San Roque families just across the frontier north of La Linea.

Copyright © Brian Hutchinson 2022

The right of Brian Hutchinson to be identified as the author of this work has been asserted by the author in accordance with sections 77 and 78 of the Copyright, Designs and Patents Act 1988.

All rights reserved. No part of this publication may be reproduced, stored in a retrieval system, or transmitted in any form or by any means, electronic, mechanical, photocopying, recording, or otherwise, without the prior permission of the publishers.

Any person who commits any unauthorised act in relation to this publication may be liable to criminal prosecution and civil claims for damages.

This is a work of fiction. Names, characters, businesses, places, events, locales, and incidents are either the products of the author's imagination or used in a fictitious manner. Any resemblance to actual persons, living or dead, or actual events is purely coincidental.

A CIP catalogue record for this title is available from the British Library.

ISBN 9781398452305 (Paperback)
ISBN 9781398452312 (ePub e-book)

www.austinmacauley.com

First Published 2022
Austin Macauley Publishers Ltd®
1 Canada Square
Canary Wharf
London
E14 5AA

20230622

Brian Hutchinson

THE GIBRALTAR CONSPIRACY

AUSTIN MACAULEY PUBLISHERS™
LONDON • CAMBRIDGE • NEW YORK • SHARJAH

Chapter 1

"How do you keep your marriage together?" Sergeant Olivier asked. "Carmen (Mrs Stagnetto) is about as Spanish as they come, and we don't really like them here?"

"Don't forget that my mother was Spanish too, if I didn't know you so well, a comment like that could well affect your promotion prospects; it's also racist, so watch it!" It was a usual humid, bad-tempered Monday morning at Police HQ.

"Sorry, sir," said Olivier with a just noticeable half smile; he liked upsetting the boss. They had worked together for nearly five years, building a relationship of trust and mutual respect that was not always evident underneath the rather spiky banter.

Fans are on full blast and making very little difference. The installation of the new air conditioning system was still not completed; the result of a brilliant cost-cutting scam in which the installer had gone bust. Albert wondered why he still lived and worked on the overcrowded Rock!

Over the weekend the rumours about a popular uprising to take over the regional government of Cadiz Province and merge with Gibraltar surfaced again. The wish to tear down the frontier controls and ease day-to-day living between La Linea and the Rock was now surprisingly strong. There was a certain tenseness in the air and Albert Stagnetto felt it, just like the humidity he hated so much.

The governor's briefing was at 11 am; they were all wondering if it would contain any further information about the people involved on both sides of the frontier.

Chapter 2

David Henley was restless; it was a hot and humid night and things were preying on his mind. David sweated a lot; they had always discussed putting air-conditioning in the flat, especially for the summer when the Levanter blows. Somehow the cash always got eaten up on other things. They really must have it done for next summer, what with David's job dictating that he spends at least six months of the year on or near Gib.

Rosemary had gone back to Winchester, with three weeks of her annual leave left. Her work seemed more important to her these days than anything else. Well, the children had all left home and were making lives of their own, quite successfully in fact.

He turned over and slipped out of bed; maybe the balcony would be cooler. He put on the low light, went to the fridge and took out a beer, opened the screen door and looked down the coast towards Gibraltar. A freshening breeze told him that the Levanter was passing, and, as he took this in, the red lights on the top of the Rock became visible. It was impressive to look from the balcony in clear weather, over the rooftops of the port at Sotogrande, 20kms down the coast to the Pillars of Hercules; Gibraltar on the European side and Cueta on the North African side and, on a good day, the Atlas Mountains in the background. The balcony of Flat 7, Bloque 'B', Torreguadiaro, had a wonderful view and you felt that you could reach out and touch the distant peaks.

(It had so impressed David on first sighting that he had picked out a new tune on his clarinet, in the style of Kenny Balls' *Midnight in Moscow*. He called it 'Gibraltar' and he thought it was good enough to record. But Rosemary and the children had never been comfortable with his musical efforts, so his embarrassment put him off ever doing anything about it. Anyway, he still liked it and frequently played it when no one else was around. One day maybe he would finish it and someone might record and release it. Dream on!)

Enough scene setting; David had a job to do. The Blair government was worried about Gibraltar's standing within the European Community. The Rock had long wished to be 'an independent state within the EC' and a financial centre to rival Hong Kong, an ambition regularly scuppered by critics including Spain and the Channel Isles who did not want Gib as a powerful rival for offshore banking. The situation had not been helped by the Barlow Clowes fiasco. In truth, Britain would love to be shot of this irritant and over-loyal territory. It seemed crazy to David that whilst the Schengen agreement had allowed the dismantling of internal borders within the main part of the European Union, to pass from Gib into Spain could face you with a delay of up to three hours on a bad day. This seemed to depend on local disputes about cigarette and drug smuggling. More often than not, on the attitude of Madrid and London, although to be fair, the hold-ups were mostly on the Spanish side.

What was the reason behind the foreign office's decision to send one of its brightest officials to work undercover to watch an unrecognised organisation operating secretly in the very south of Spain? An action which, if discovered, would harm Anglo-Spanish relations for years to come. There was a feeling in the region that something had to be resolved soon. Maybe it was spurred on by the smooth hand-over of Hong Kong to China in 1997, but the Gibraltar situation was now unique and a focal point for criticism of past British colonial rule. When viewed from a distance, the possible solutions seemed obvious and simple. Why not a joint assembly such as that have exists in Andorra between France and Spain? But the closer you got to the problem the more complicated and difficult it appeared.

He showered and dressed quickly. He was to meet Jose Gomez, a local lawyer and Andalusian activist, in the Ke Bar at Puerto Sotogrande. The weather had improved and it was a fine morning; coffee outside would be welcome. He did not know why Gomez wanted to meet him and was concerned that maybe his cover had been blown.

He walked along the shoreline towards the port; the sun was hot and bright, making the white buildings appear starker than usual. He had not met Gomez before but recognised him immediately from a photograph he had seen in last week's local rag. Jose Medrano Gomez was a fine-looking man, not overweight but quite stocky in build. He had a fine nose and high forehead and was uniformly suntanned. He looked every bit the fortyish and wealthy polo player.

David did not have to approach Gomez and introduce himself, as Gomez was at once on his feet. "Mr Henley, what a pleasure, join me for coffee; I take mine cortado –just cut with milk."

"Yes, that will do me nicely, what a beautiful morning," David replied. They sat at an outside table, there was a light breeze and the sun still had some strength. The port at Soto had been very exclusive, but now it seemed to be taking on a bit of the spirit of Banus, laddish and loads a money, with all the new high-rise developments competing price-wise. Not a clever move.

"Shall I come straight to the point?" said Gomez. "I know that you are an undersecretary with the FCO, but I do not know why you are here, in Spain, and not in Gibraltar where they desperately need your help. Do they know you are here?"

"Not officially," said David, "they think I am on leave. I don't know what help they could possibly want from me, Gibraltar treats we Brits more like the enemy than your local Spanish these days."

"That's why I am so glad that we meet today. May I call you David; it makes things so much friendlier?" David nodded approval, although he could not bring himself, as yet, to address Gomez by his first name.

"I have a Gibraltarian cousin," Gomez said, and he went on to tell David how their fathers, as brothers, had to make a choice about nationality during the Second World War. The brothers Gomez were of an age to be conscripted into the military whichever side they chose to support. It was likely that Spain would join the Axis powers, and Gib was a British Base. "My cousin Philippo is a member of the Gibraltar Government, and through him, I know much of what is going on there, we are very close you know. He is as disillusioned with London as I am with our Government in Madrid."

Gomez went on to tell how, contrary to the general perception; there was a strengthening bond between the ordinary citizens of Gibraltar and La Linea. This was based upon ancient family ties around the Campo de Gibraltar and extended into much of adjacent Andalusia. He alluded to contacts with powerful Hong Kong financiers and the Sultan of Borogi. "We have the means and the friends to be financially independent as a region Mr Henley." He dropped the over-friendly David, this was a serious matter. "Imagine a new member of the European Community, made up of much of southern Andalusia plus Gibraltar; a real economic force to be reckoned with! Think about it and we'll discuss it in more detail next time we meet. But please, please keep it to yourself for the time being. I am very tight for time today and I must leave now as I have another meeting on a quite different matter. Polo is my second greatest love, but it is very expensive. However, I have a very wealthy and beautiful sponsor, you must meet her sometime. But I must warn you, she is very demanding."

With that, he stood up, gave a slight bow and was gone, leaving David to pay the bill! What should he make of it all; Gomez had implied so much and said so little. He also seemed unreal, a dreamer with an inflated view of his own importance. His boasts of a strong allegiance with Gibraltar did not quite ring true, after all, Bossano hated the Spanish and always made that quite clear when he was the first minister on the Rock.

The only way to find out the reality of the situation was to go to Gib, but this posed a problem for David Henley as he was not officially supposed to be here.

Chapter 3

Albert Stagnetto left the briefing and made for his house at 44a Main Street. It was 1.15 pm and time for lunch and a siesta. There were no cruise ships in Gib today, so the walk down Main Street was swifter than usual, with no large Americans, Germans and Dutch to impede his progress. Carmen was out today, fundraising for her favourite charity, so he would have to fend for himself. He was no longer allowed his favourite foods; pasta and rice were definitely out on the Atkins diet. At 5ft 8 ins he had always felt comfortable at a weight of 15 stone. But Carmen had said he was becoming lethargic and, at 55, he should take more care; a kind way of suggesting he was overweight and needed to slim down. He had taken her comment very seriously, and on the carbohydrate-free regime had shed over a stone in five weeks. The target was 12 stone and he really felt it was achievable.

The ground floor at 44 Main Street was occupied by Carlos Brothers' Camera and Stereo shop. The entrance to the upstairs accommodation was through a door to the right of the window display. He opened the door and was immediately struck by the cool and pleasant air, quite a change from police HQ and the governor's office.

The accommodation was spread over three floors of the four-storey building; the first floor comprised a sitting room and dining room/kitchen, on the second floor was a study, their master bedroom and bathroom, and on the third floor their daughter's bedroom and a guest room.

When they were first married they shared the house with his parents, his father had started the electrical business on the ground floor after the Second World War and sold it to the Carlos Brothers when he retired, realising that Albert was set on joining the British Army, a natural step towards the police. Following the deaths of his parents (within three months of each other) they inherited the building and continued to live above the shop, receiving a useful rent income from the business.

A 'post-it' note on the fridge told him that Carmen had left some cold pork, celery and manchego cheese on the top shelf for his lunch. He grabbed it and went to the table. Today's copy of the Gibraltar Chronicle caught his eye; the headline read: "Gomez Accused of Soft Attitude Towards Spain." He read on with interest and quickly concluded that the journalist was speculating rather than basing his front-page story on facts; facts that would be hard to come by.

The meeting that morning in the governor's office was also based on speculation, but a serious air had pervaded the proceedings; there's no smoke without fire was the general belief.

Chapter 4

David Henley decided that he would be less conspicuous if he was smartly dressed and business-like. Recently both the Spanish and Gibraltarian border police had a purge on scruffy-looking individuals, and he could not afford to be noticed. He also decided to drive to the frontier, park the Spanish-registered car and cross on foot. It was a Monday, and when he saw the queue of cars stretching westwards way past the new roundabout, he was glad that he had decided to walk over. Finding a parking bay by the brown flats, the first modern symbol erected by Franco to be viewed from Gibraltar; and also a great vantage point for his special police with their powerful binoculars to watch the comings and goings at the border, he approached the pay and display machine.

The friendly Spanish parking warden helped him with change at the machine. It was a nice morning, but he had a sinking feeling that he was getting involved in a situation that could turn out to be very uncomfortable indeed. The Rock had a small lid of cloud sitting on its western edge, but the rest of the sky was a brilliant clear blue. He crossed the dual carriageway and passed the long line of cars waiting to enter the territory. Everyone seemed relaxed and there was no hint of the tension which sometimes built up at this strange frontier. He even got a smile from the Spanish border policeman, who just took a cursory glance at the dog-eared passport as he passed. Now he was through the Spanish gates and, in the distance, could see the British-style policeman's helmet sitting on the desk next to the officer on duty. David prepared to flash his passport at the officer. This was the usual practice, just a glance and a wave, but not today!

"Excuse me, sir, may I inspect your passport?"

"Yes, of course. Is there a problem?"

"No, sir, no problem; you are Mr Henley?"

"Yes."

"Would you mind waiting in the office for a few moments, sir, just a formality? It's just down the corridor on the right, before the customs office."

David had never been stopped or questioned before and was beginning to feel just a little uncomfortable. Somehow one expects to be suspect when crossing into foreign territory, but Gib is so very British, this was not right.

The office door was open and he went in. There was a hint of cigar smoke, it seemed familiar.

"Good morning, Mr Henley, how nice to meet you." It was Gomez, but not Jose Gomez; therefore, it must be Philippo. The likeness was uncanny; he could have been Jose's twin. "I am so sorry to interrupt your smooth passage to our Rock; I know how embarrassing it can be for someone such as yourself to have his credentials questioned. However, it is necessary as we need to talk urgently. I have a car waiting, so please join me in more comfortable surroundings." He led the way out of the interrogation room to a large black Toyota Land Cruiser with darkened windows. It was parked on the double yellow line and its driver was in deep conversation with a policeman who, on seeing Philippo Gomez, stepped back and gave a half-salute.

"Sergeant Olivier, how nice to see you," said Gomez. "How are Angelica and your beautiful children, they are well, I hope?"

"Minister, they are very well and are visiting her family in Malta for two weeks." The sergeant beamed, expertly covering his intense dislike of this self-serving and dangerous man; it was good for intelligence gathering to remain on friendly terms with such a charismatic politician.

The driver started the engine, and Gomez ushered David into the back seat of the Land cruiser; Sergeant Olivier saluted once more, and they were off.

"Life is full of the unexpected; my cousin Jose phoned to say that he had met you today," said Philippo. "He thought you and I should talk soon before the Gibraltar Government knows officially that you are here."

"But you are part of the government here, surely you are not the only one to know of my presence in Spain; how did you know I was coming to Gib today, are you having me followed?" David was alarmed.

"Not exactly, but we attached a small tracking device to your rented car, which causes a transponder to bleep in my office here when you are within four kilometres of the Rock. It bleeped an hour ago, so I was able to ask Sergeant Olivier to hold you gently at the frontier until I arrived. You were in fact slower than I anticipated and I got here first."

"I had difficulty with the pay and display machine when I parked in La Linea," said David.

"Yes, they can be tricky, I know. We really should have a common currency between brothers and sisters on either side of this ridiculous divide. Do I surprise you, do you share in the misconception that we Gibraltarians hate and despise our neighbouring La Lineans? We are all one family you know; we are all, in fact, Andalusians."

The Land Cruiser had crossed the airstrip, turned right at the roundabout and stopped in the car park at Marina Bay. It felt so strange to be driving on the right when all the road signs were identical to those in the UK. He thought for a moment that he was being taken to Da Paulo, the excellent restaurant frequented by the great and the good of Gibraltar. But no, they just sat in the car; David felt hot and uncomfortable.

"Are you telling me that there might be an informal arrangement between Gibraltar and Spain at a very local level?"

"Not so very local, I prefer to say regional. Just listen to the Spanish we speak on the Rock; then listen to the Spanish spoken, not just in La Linea but in Andalusia generally. It is almost identical, unlike the Spanish spoken in Madrid. We are a region, just as Catalonia and the Basque Country are identifiable regions. It is my personal belief that the government in Madrid uses the Gibraltar question to disguise its real worry, which is that Andalusia will one-day demand independence from Madrid. It is a larger area than Scotland and has many more people and great hidden wealth. We are also a very proud people, proud of our unique identity."

David noticed Philippo Gomez becoming more and more excited as he painted the picture of an independent Andalusia which included Gibraltar. He could not really believe his ears, it was a scenario never dreamt of, and yet, in a strange way, it made very good sense. His problem was now twofold, to believe him and, if so, how to handle it with the FCO. It was dynamite so far as Anglo-Spanish relations were concerned, but a very tempting way for the UK to rid itself of the recurring Gibraltar headaches.

Chapter 5
A Period of Reflection

Philippo Gomez dropped David by the old Safeway building opposite the airfield control tower; not wanting the Spanish border police, surveying the British side with powerful binoculars, to see them together. He crossed the road and went to the airport shop to buy the Times. The airport had improved a lot since the reopening of the frontier in 1982; the original RAF buildings had given way to proper commercial facilities. It was, however, a shame that a sensible deal with Spain could not be concluded so that incoming visitors could choose to clear either Gibraltarian or Spanish immigration and customs controls. Nowadays, most of the tourists coming into Gibraltar cross immediately into Spain, but it meant clearing Gib customs and then walking across the frontier to clear Spanish customs. Very time-consuming and tiring, especially in the heat. It had always amused David's family that the airport is run by a company called Terminal Management, not a name he would have chosen!

He left the airport and walked towards the frontier; there were a few cars queuing at the Spanish control point, but nobody seemed bothered today. Showing his passport, he was waved on; crossing the dual carriageway, he found the car.

Now to locate the tracker; he felt underneath the rear bumper, and the small magnetic device came away easily. How dare they do this to him; he looked around and noticed a Policia Local patrol car parked outside McDonald's, engine running and no one at the controls. It was a risk, but he thought it worth it, as he attached the magnet underneath the police car's rear end. *'That'll teach them,'* he thought gleefully. Then he was back in his own hire car heading back towards Sotogrande and the flat in Torreguadiaro.

Driving carefully along the new road he mulled over in his mind the strength of Philippo Gomez's vision, it still seemed like a fantasy. All the years of aggression and posturing between the UK and Spain; Gibraltar cast the boil on the beautiful body. Surely the prejudices were too firmly entrenched to allow such a visionary outcome as suggested by the Gomez cousins?

The message light was flashing on the answerphone in the flat; he pressed the replay button. Two messages to call London, another from Rosemary to say she had arrived home safely, and the last one from Señora Salsun saying she would call him again later. He was tired and irritable, enough work for one day. He made for Rio Seco.

Chapter 6

Albert Stagnetto woke from an anxious siesta. He remembered a time in the not-too-distant past when he could just switch off, sleep soundly for an hour and awake refreshed; not any more it seemed. Too much caffeine, no carbohydrates to give that burst of energy, and just his work to concentrate on these days. He was sure his family loved him; but did they need him anymore? What was his domestic role these days; provider of income and very little else? Don't dwell on it, he thought. A quick shower while the coffee brewed, then back into the fray.

He walked briskly up Main Street, nodding occasionally to those he recognised. Not stopping as he usually did to talk to anyone; he wanted to get to the bottom of this annoying conspiracy theory, so no room in his head for other thoughts. One of the participants at the governor's meeting this morning had hinted that a senior British diplomat was lurking around the Campo de Gibraltar, the Spanish territory where La Linea and San Roque were the major towns. What he was doing there was a mystery, but the source had hinted that a member of the Gibraltar Government, a minister no less, with strong family links to Spain, had met 'unofficially' with this faceless British public servant.

His office was unbearably humid; some interfering busybody had turned off his fan as per the energy-saving order. Why couldn't people mind their own business? He dug deep into his memory; which minister had close relatives across the frontier? The only one he knew was Gomez, the trade minister; Philippo Gomez; PG as he was known to friends and foes alike. In Albert's opinion, he was the most difficult and untrustworthy member of the current administration, with a very high media profile and a violent temper. These criticisms were generally accepted, but in Albert Stagnetto's case, it was more to do with *two* facts: fact one, Albert had investigated the alleged corruption charge that Gomez had taken substantial backhanders when he was a minister in charge of funding the refurbishment of Police HQ. It had come to nothing, but only due to the investigation being starved of manpower, on instruction from the Chief Constable. It had also been hinted very strongly to the then-young Stagnetto that his career path might end up as the road to nowhere if he insisted on pursuing the matter! Fact two was more of a personal nature; Gomez, in a drunken state, had made a pass at Mrs Stagnetto during last year's official Christmas reception at the governor's residence.

Chapter 7
Unexpected Meeting

Rio Seco was run by Pepe and was a large restaurant overlooking the beach next to Bloque B. Pepe had been part of the local glamour as a young man. He ran the first disco in Torreguadiaro in the late 1970s and had ambitions to become a radio DJ. He had now matured in years and was a father of three, still a handsome man if a little overweight. He greeted David with a smile and a firm handshake, he was a kind and very solid person. Quite often, when the children, who were now old enough to take holidays independently, came down, Pepe would keep a distant eye on them. When they inevitably ran out of money he would feed them and advance a little cash. David would repay this debt whenever he turned up, it was an easy relationship. Pepe never allowed the Henleys to speak Spanish with him, his command of English was good enough to discourage any attempt.

"You look tired," he said when David entered the bar and offered a Malaga Wine and Soda.

David nodded and Pepe produced it along with some real black olives. (Did you know that most black olives we buy in the UK are green ones dyed black? I didn't know. It is olive fraud!). "What do you think of Gibraltar, Pepe?" David asked.

Pepe thought for a moment and said that he could not understand why it was perceived as such a problem. The people there were generally friendly, they spoke Spanish and English. There were a few troublemakers, but generally, the differences were blown up out of proportion to satisfy the egos of remote politicians in London and Madrid. Not quite the Gomez line, but not that different.

Still sitting at the bar, David had Sopa de mariscos followed by a tortilla. Pepe's sopa was famous all along the coast between Estapona and La Linea. He asked Pepe about the road. The Autovia, a Spanish motorway, was almost complete between Malaga and Algeciras. It was supposed to be completed totally for the 1997 Ryder Cup at Valderrama, but Malaga Province ran out of money. So, the most dangerous stretch of road in Spain ran right through the middle of Torreguadiaro. From the western side of Estepona through to the Guadiaro River Bridge, it was a narrow two-way road that had claimed 18 lives within a two-year period. Huge articulated lorries thundered through all day and all night and most locals prayed for the completion of the Autovia soon. "Maybe the road will be finished before the year 2000, and maybe it won't. My business will suffer when we are bypassed, but that is a small price to pay for saving local lives. But you know, there is a strange reluctance amongst local officials in Cadiz Province to put pressure on Malaga Province to complete their part of the new road. I think there is more going on than we are told." I could tell from the look he gave me that there was more he would like to say, but he stopped abruptly.

He asked David why he was here, for a holiday, saying that he was not usually in Torreguadiaro at this time of the year.

"I have a little job to do, Pepe," David replied.

"With a dangerous woman." A wry smile spread over his suntanned face. He was looking over David's shoulder towards the door. David looked up into the mirror behind the bar and saw the reflection of Anna Marie Salsun approaching from behind him.

She was an extraordinary-looking woman, small and neat in appearance. Her youthful looks belied her age; some say she was on the wrong side of fifty. She was dark-skinned, as one would expect for an Argentinean, but she had the most piercing blue eyes and very blond hair.

They had met socially on a few occasions during the polo season at Sotogrande. The last time was in the summer when John Taylor, who owned the largest and most profitable real estate business in Soto, offered his usual corporate hospitality. His company sponsored several match cups and David and Rosemary had a thrilling evening watching dangerously fast polo. He knew that Anna Marie was friendly with John's wife Sue and that she had put some of her vast personal fortune behind his new reality business.

"David Henley, how nice to see you. I would say you've been avoiding me if I did not know that you were a perfect gentleman." There was just a slight hint of sarcasm and accent in her voice, but otherwise, her English was perfect and almost upper-class. "Anna Marie, how good to see you, I got your message on the answerphone when I returned from Gib, about an hour ago. I was going to call you this evening, but you have beaten me to it; I didn't know there was any urgency."

"Life has an urgency for me since Augusto died," she replied. "So much to do and so little time to achieve anything meaningful." Her late husband Augusto de Souzacruz- Salsun was the highest-ranking ambassador in the Argentinean diplomatic service. His last posting was to Madrid where sadly he died after being crushed by his polo pony. He was admired for the stance he took following the Falklands invasion and subsequent Argentinean defeat. This quiet admiration even extended to the FCO in London, where he had become the main source of contact as Britain and Argentina attempted to repair their damaged relationship. He was responsible for the soft line taken by Spain during the Falklands War when it was tempting for Spain to side with the South Americans and cite Gibraltar as yet another colonial outpost of a dying empire. Gibraltar, Gibraltar; it was cropping up again and again!

"Pepe, a whisky and water for Señora Salsun, and remember, no ice." Another of Anna Marie's quirks, she loved Scotch and would drink it even in the hottest weather. She took the glass and sipped at the contents.

"You are not here on a pleasure trip I gather, no Rosemary and no children?" She seemed to be closely examining him with those strange clear blue eyes.

"I won't pretend to you," he replied. "I am here on unofficial business, but everyone seems to know that, on both sides of the frontier."

"Oh, you mean those delightful Gomez boys; there is not much that they don't know. Sometimes I think they are too clever for their own good, but they are amusing don't you think?"

I thought I detected a hint of sarcasm in her voice, she finished her drink. Pepe had gone into the restaurant to take an order for dinner; there were just the two of them in the bar.

"You know about their plans for Andalusia-Gibraltar?" The clarity of her question was quite shocking; he paused before responding.

"I had heard rumours, after all, that is why the FCO has sent me here, but I did not take it seriously at first. You know, all that old baggage about Gibraltarian independence and the mutual 'hate' between the Rock and Spain."

"I think there is far more going on than we might imagine, even in our wildest dreams," she said. "I am also aware of this so-called conspiracy; for this part of Cadiz Province to secede from Spain and link with Gibraltar. I don't know how it would be achieved, but it would certainly require the support of a great many powerful people and a great deal of cash. One of the rumours is that the Sultan of Borogi, along with some Hong Kong financiers would open a sufficiently large line of credit to support a new state. Do you know that it is Sultan's money that is behind much of the development around here and not that of the late President Marcos? The Borogi royal family is large and expensive and they would love to have something more than just an official base here."

"Why are you sharing this with me, Anna Marie? It's all so speculative, where is the proof, the reality?"

David thought carefully for a moment, they were both silent as Pepe fussed behind the bar and then retreated into the kitchen.

"What do you want me to relay to my masters in London?"

"Nothing yet," she said, "but I would like you to meet a few more people before you decide whether this is for real or not."

David felt numb, too much to take in, in one day. He asked Pepe for the bill, paid in cash, and Anna Marie left the Rio Seco and headed for the port at Sotogrande.

Chapter 8

Albert Stagnetto picked up his phone. "Can you get me my brother-in-law in San Roque please Maria?" His secretary, Maria Jones, had been his loyal supporter for many years, knew most of Albert's family's numbers off by heart and, in less than a minute, he was connected to Ramon at the Hacienda in San Roque. "Alberto, how are you?" Ramon was the only member of his wife's family allowed to use 'Alberto'; to everyone else, he was always just Albert.

"I'm fine, a little fraught today; tell me, have you picked up a hint of this conspiracy to create an independent Andalusia to include Gibraltar?" There was a brief silence, then a chuckle "Only every year for the past ten years; which nutter is it this time?"

"It could be a pair of very powerful and dangerous nutters Ramon, one close to the centre of our present Gibraltar Government, the other just as dangerous and powerful on your side of the frontier; they and their ambitions could cause a major diplomatic crisis if allowed to develop any further."

"The name Gomez wouldn't by any chance be connected with this?" said Ramon. "The cousin on this side of the fence is causing a lot of grief by leaking his grandiose plans for this union between Andalusia and Gibraltar. The old family feuds cannot just be wiped out with a pair of wire cutters and the funding requirement would be enormous; it's a truly crazy idea. There must be big, big money in this for the Gomez cousins, it's not only the power they are keen on; they never do anything unless there's a great deal of cash involved."

"It's very tricky for me Ramon, my sergeant, James Olivier, is aware that Philippo Gomez is up to something." Albert went on to describe how Sgt Olivier had been called personally at home by Gomez and instructed to detain David Henley at the frontier until he, Philippo, arrived. He was told that it would be beneficial to his career prospects in the police if this were to be a secret between them. The arrogance and stupidity of the man to even think that James Olivier would not share this experience with his close colleagues!

"I know nothing of any David Henley; who is he?" Ramon Lopez was more than just a little curious. "Could he be the British diplomat, on gardening leave here in Spain?"

"Ramon, please believe me when I tell you that I know nothing of this man except that Philippo Gomez has a great interest in him. Sergeant Olivier told me that the Gomez cousins had attached a tracking device to Henley's Spanish hire car, just to keep tabs on him, that's how Philippo knew when he was about to arrive at the frontier."

"That's interesting Alberto, one of my patrol cars has been of major interest, you know, being followed or met in very out-of-the-way places by men with dark glasses. I had the vehicle checked out; what did we discover, a tracking device just like you describe! The men in dark glasses had very red faces when they found out their device was in a

Spanish police car. I think Mr Henley has a sense of humour-no?"

There was a pause in the conversation whilst both men tried to stifle their laughter.

Albert broke the silence. "I also have this personal difficulty, in that Philippo made a pass at Carmen at the governor's Christmas party last year, and I am desperately trying to keep my personal feelings about him under control. Frankly, if I'm honest with you, I would love to see him fall from a great height, metaphorically speaking of course!"

Albert had the feeling that as he slowly removed large stones, he was discovering some really nasty and dangerous reptiles underneath. He thanked Ramon, and they agreed to meet for dinner the following week to catch up on any new moves and hung up.

Chapter 9
The Sultan's Man

Bobby Tweed was six feet three inches tall. As a young man, he had been extremely slim, which had made him look even taller than he was. Now, however, the good life had got to him just a bit too much and he was decidedly paunchy.

Bobby had been at Emanuel School in London where he shared a classroom with one of the Sultan of Borogi's nephews; he had always been a sharp operator but was academically poor. So was the young prince, and they became firm friends. As neither was destined for university, Bobby found himself working in Borogi as the prince's gofer, court jester and constant companion. He received a huge, by UK standards, tax-free salary plus numerous gifts including a Series 7 BMW which he wrote off doing excessive speeds on the only bit of dual-carriageway in Borogi. He travelled to all the glamorous places in the world with the Prince, and then one day decided that he needed a proper job. The young prince's father, brother to the Sultan, suggested that Bobby should manage their investment in Sotogrande.

So, some two years later he was well established as the minder of the royal money, living in extreme luxury in a vast villa, with the use of a large yacht, and membership at Valderama. He was seated at an end table in the Ke Bar and stood up as we approached.

"Hi, Anna, how's life?"

"Oh, a little less boring day by day, thanks, Bobby. This is my good friend David Henley; he needs convincing that we are not all completely mad when we talk about the 'project.' I thought you might give him a hint as to your backers' views?"

"Let's sit and have a drink," said Bobby. "Our view is very positive, we have major investments here in Spain which we wish to preserve and to grow even bigger. We would not consider supporting such a major event if it did not have the wholesale support of the majority of local people on both sides of the frontier. We also believe that, in time, it will have the support of both the Spanish and British Governments. The new territory could even become a member of the Commonwealth!" He laughed, Borogi was very proud of its long links with the Commonwealth.

"You know, Gib always strived to become an independent state within the European Community, the Rock has been flying the blue stars EU flag for many years now. If the way forward for Gib in the EC is helped by linking up with this independent part of Spain, then why not bury all the past prejudices?"

They continued the discussion for about two hours; the strong message from Bobby Tweed was that his master's involvement could only proceed with the tacit support of the UK and Spanish Governments.

David began to think the unthinkable; he also noticed that Anna Marie was becoming restless. She had made it quite clear that she and Bobby had other business to take care of, the business of a more intimate nature. Being a trained diplomat, David had picked up on this quite early in the evening. "It's getting late," he said, "and I have some calls to make."

He thanked Anna Marie for her kindness in introducing him to Bobby, shook Bobby's hand, kissed Anna on each cheek and left. As they had arrived in her car, he decided to walk back along the beach to Torreguadiaro.

Crazy though it seemed, he wanted to see a map of this new territory. How far would it extend? Jose Gomez had talked about the whole of Andalusia, but David felt it would be far more local and focused around the Campo de Gibraltar. Letting himself into the flat, he took a cold beer from the fridge, picked up a map from the bookshelf, and went out onto the balcony. It was a clear night, the sea was calm and silent, and Gib was clearly visible. He sat down and unfolded the map.

Many places in southern Andalusia followed their name with 'de la Frontera.' Jimena de la Frontera was the one he knew best, but there were many more. They marked the boundary of the Moorish invasion when the coastal part of southern Spain was ruled by the Moors for some 700 years between AD 711 and AD 1462. Would this line of 'Frontera' towns become the new boundary for a new territory? Would it include Cadiz, he didn't think so. But if you followed the map to the west from Gibraltar, then Algiceras and Tarifa would be included. Wasn't there a Frontera town just north of that wonderful stretch of beach at Bolonia; that would ideally mark the western extreme? What about the eastern boundary, perhaps Estapona, it was still very Spanish and unspoiled, but it was in Malaga Province where, beyond Estapona, the once poor and small coastal towns had become holiday resorts on a grand scale, San Pedro, Puerto Banus, Fuengirola, and Marbella. Somehow, he could not imagine their inclusion in this plan. He was also certain that Malaga would be excluded, it was too big and it was already somewhat independent in its own way.

David put on his reading glasses and studied the map. The place name he could not remember was Vejer de la Frontera, but a little further north on the coast was Conil de la Frontera. Drawing a line inland from there and north was Medina Sidonia, then across to Jimena de la Frontera and back south down to San Diego on the coast road between Sotogrande and Estapona. San Diego marked the boundary between Cadiz Province and Malaga Province on the dangerous piece of two-way coastal strip road that, at that time, linked the Autovia at Sotogrande with the Autovia at Estapona. The Moors had got it right; it was an ideally defensible territory, with plentiful water supplies and very fertile land.

If this was the Gomez scenario, then he could see why they were so confident and excited about their plan. It was then that David determined to confront them the next day and clarify the extent of their support.

Chapter 10
The Real Picture

David contacted Jose Gomez. At first, he was reluctant to take the call, something big was being planned, and he had no time for pointless meetings. His attitude changed, however, when David told him that he had informally raised the matter with London. Would he meet him the next evening at the Hostel Anon in Jimena; come alone and expect to meet some surprising people?

David had not yet contacted London, so he put a call in straight away. The story he related to the Permanent Secretary came as no surprise. The only bit of information the PS didn't have was knowledge of tomorrow's meeting. David demanded to know the real reason why he had been posted to Spain when the FCO already knew of the conspiracy. The terse reply was that he had been sent to Spain to confirm all that was going on, and that had he kept in regular contact with the head of the unit, he would have been put in the picture earlier.

Asked what stance Madrid would take if and when the plan crystallised, he said there would be a lot of loud noises, accusations and hot air, but that Spain would not resort to force to quell a democratic uprising. Anyhow, most of the law enforcers in southern Andalusia were behind the move, so who would stop it, not riot police from Madrid?

Amazingly, it seemed to David Henley that a lot of work had been going on secretly behind the scenes for years and that he was about to witness the beginning of its culmination.

Chapter 11

Carmen Stagnetto busied herself in the kitchen, their daughter was out with friends; she had said something about going to a nightclub in Banus. Carmen had been tempted to say that illegal substances were easily available in Gibraltar or in La Linea and Sotogrande, so why go all the way to Banus, but she had thought better of it.

Antonia swore on her life that she was not into drugs; neither were her friends, but it was difficult to believe. Carmen found her main job these days was to keep the peace between Albert and Antonia. Strange really, because up to a year ago there was such a strong bond between them, so strong in fact that Carmen often felt the odd one out. Not any longer, however, since Antonia's 17th birthday things had got really bad; Albert wanted to know exactly where his daughter was, with whom, and when would she be home. "But Dad, I'm seventeen now; my friends' parents don't keep tabs on their daughters like you do on me; why can't you trust me, why can't you leave me alone? This protest, like so many others recently, echoed in Carmen's mind; could she do anything to ease the situation, or would her efforts just make things worse?"

Overture

David Henley spent a relaxing morning, rising late and strolling down to the port for breakfast. Sotogrande was deserted, it felt like an unused film set. Apart from the Ke Bar, all the restaurants had closed for the winter. Sitting there admiring all the marine real estate, he noticed Anna's friend and business partner John Taylor walking towards his office. He called to him and he turned; he must have been very short-sighted, he frowned and stared blankly in David's direction.

"John, it's me, David Henley."

"David, good to see you, sorry I looked puzzled but I've lost my glasses, can't see a bloody thing without them."

He asked him to join him for coffee and he seemed pleased to accept. "How are you, how's the new business?"

"Not so good; too many of us set up in Soto, chasing too little business. However, I hope to survive; Anna has promised to fund me until we are established. She's very supportive and very rich."

David felt slightly embarrassed that John Taylor had felt it necessary to mention Anna's wealth so casually, maybe he was just grateful to her. That set him wondering about her relationship with Bobby Tweed, Sultan's man, who was so much younger than her. But he was very wealthy too, so perhaps she could only be truly relaxed knowing that her partner was not after her money. David had come across many wealthy people, thrown together because of their riches and excluding more suitable partners because of their cash paranoia.

He wanted to know if John was aware of today's meeting, and whether he had been invited, but he did not want to ask outright.

"It seems very quiet all along the Costa right now?"

John shrugged his shoulders. "I guess things might liven up a bit after today's meeting, are you going?" he asked.

No point in lying, so I told him I was. He was a supporter of the initiative and said that he hoped all the players would turn up. If they did, then there was a real chance of it going ahead quite soon. He was concerned that all the mayors from the 'Frontera' towns and villages in the immediate region should attend.

"We have all the financial muscle and tacit diplomatic support we need," he said, "but without the support of the ordinary people of both territories, we don't stand a chance."

David agreed about this, John was fairly certain of support on the Spanish side of the frontier but personally did not trust the Gibraltarians to shape up.

Chapter 12
The Meeting

They were to meet in Jimena de la Frontera at 7 pm under the guise of the Regional Chamber of Commerce, the only officially recognised cross-border organisation.

David left the flat, drove up the slope from the car park and waited some four minutes before safely turning left towards San Roque. He passed the turning to the port at Soto, then past the huge Ceramica to the new roundabout at the beginning of the recently completed Autovia. It was there that he turned inland through San Enrique to San Martin de Tesorillo; very fertile farmland with orange groves on both sides of the road. The sky had a watery Turnerish look about it, he was feeling decidedly nervous about the immediate future.

After about twenty minutes he reached the T junction of the main road to Jimena, it looked strangely deserted. He turned right and increased speed, it was one of those newly tarred and cambered roads, rebuilt with EC money; the Junta de Andalusia had done very well by Brussels. On either side of the road were cork oak trees, most of which had been stripped of their valuable bark. Up to the left was the old white town of Casteliar which Franco had ordered to become uninhabited once he had built the very unattractive new town of Nuevo Casteliar in the fertile valley. The old town had overnight become home to all the 1970s hippies in Southern Spain, most of them from Holland and Germany. The authorities tried in vain to shift them but today many of the residents are the children and grandchildren of those original squatters.

The road sign read Estacion Jimena, and I passed through the satellite of Jimena proper which had grown up around the railway station. A little further on, past the huge dairy which now provided Fresco Leche del Dia for all the British ex-pats to have in their morning tea. It was also available at Safeway on Gibraltar, another sign of the barriers coming down. A left turn off the main road, and up the steep slope to the old town of Jimena de la Frontera.

The Hostel Anon was almost at the highest point in the town, beneath the old castle. It was made up of adjoining small houses which had been knocked together. It was very tastefully furnished and, from memory, the beds were very comfortable. It was owned and managed by Anna, an American woman, whose husband had tragically died some years after they opened the hotel. He had been born in East Africa where his family farmed. He was sent off to boarding school, and to get there he travelled by train. The whole of the hotel walls were covered in wonderful monochrome photos of steam trains, odd to find such a collection in the southern mountains of Spain.

There was a notice in the lobby announcing the meeting of the Chambers of Commerce of Southern Spain and Gibraltar. It was in the main dining room and would take place at 8 pm, followed by dinner. It was now 7.30 pm, and delegates were starting to arrive. I made my way up to the roof garden, I needed some fresh air and to gather my thoughts.

The view from the roof was spectacular, the evening was clear and the sun had just dropped behind hills. In the far distance, I could make out the faint outline of Gibraltar. Strangely, it seemed visible from wherever you were in this part of Spain.

Always there, always reminding us of its permanence and mankind's transience. I helped myself to a beer from the fridge, wrote down what I had, and sat down. I could hear people arriving downstairs and the excited buzz of conversation and greetings increased. I finished the beer, stood up took in a large breath of the cool evening air, and made my way downstairs.

The Chambers' secretary had laid out a table with lapel badges, and a list of delegates and a seating plan had been pinned up on a board. Newly arriving delegates were greeting each other warmly in Spanish. Many wore dress regalia, signifying that they were mayors of local Frontera towns, all were smartly dressed. They huddled in groups of three or four, I recognised local faces from San Enrique, San Martin and Guadiaro. At the far end of the lobby was a larger group that included the Gomez cousins, Bobby Tweed and Inspector Stagnetto of the Gibraltar police. There were no women present, so it was to be really serious business discussed tonight.

I consulted the table plans. Someone must have thought very hard about this, as the groups had been effectively split up so that as many delegates as possible sat next to those they didn't know, a true melting pot.

"Hombres Simpaticos." A small rotund man wearing a mayoral chain was beaming at the gathering. "It is time to begin this historic meeting, a meeting long overdue, a meeting whose outcome tonight will change, for the better of us all, this unique part of our beloved Andalusia. Many of you are strangers to each other now, but at the end of the evening we shall all recognise ourselves for the brothers that we are, one large family with a single purpose to unite and develop to its true potential, this new territory. The seating plans ensure that you do not sit in familiar groups, but with strangers who, by the end of the evening will be strangers no longer."

"We shall discuss, in-depth, the detailed plans and timing of the coordinated move to join Los Fronteras and Gibraltar, at the same time separating forever from the rest of Spain. This will be done with no bloodshed, quietly, efficiently and with honour. The civil guard and traffic police are, to a man, solidly behind this action. The Gibraltar police are also in agreement and will become part of a new joint law enforcement agency." He glanced at Inspector Stagnetto who beamed at him. A new currency, the Sterletta, will be issued over a five-day period following the establishment of our new union.

"The only weapons we use will be wire cutters to dismantle the frontier fence at La Linea/Gibraltar, and we will erect road barriers at San Diego on the N340 at KM 145, Fuente del Gallo on the N340 at Km 80, Medina Sidona on the C346, Alcala de los Gazules on the A381, and here at Jimena de la Frontera on the C333 1. We do not intend to interrupt the flow of traffic between our new territory and Spain, that would not be in the spirit of Shengen*. We will only use the barriers in the unlikely event of any military action by our new neighbour Spain! Hombres, Hermanos, let us begin."

An Inspector Calls, maybe?

"I want you to get over there right away Stagnetto, the whole thing is getting out of control," the governor's spokesman was shouting down the phone which Albert held away from his ear. *'What the hell does he think I can do,'* thought Albert, fried egg and bacon sandwich in one hand (not on the Atkins diet), phone in the other hand. The meeting's happening in Spain, it's been planned for months, and the Spanish and English know it's going on; what was he supposed to do?

"I'm sorry Maurice, but I daren't interfere, it is not a Gibraltar police matter, there is no crime being committed, not yet anyhow, and it is not on our territory."

"Yes, it damn well is; well it's been planned on Gibraltar by that bloody Gomez. The governor's got a bad case of cold feet; he thought it had the tacit approval of the foreign office, but they are now vehemently denying any prior knowledge. It's worse than a failed coup, and heads will roll."

'Whose heads,' thought Albert, *'what a mess.'*

Chapter 13
Implementation

There were no written minutes taken at the Jimena meeting, but it was unanimously agreed that New Year's Day 2004 would be La Frontera Day. It would be preceded on December 31 by a 'Hands Across the Border' celebration in La Linea and Gibraltar to which the European Commissioner for Schengen would be the guest of honour. His presence would guarantee, in as much as anything can be guaranteed, that the 'celebrations' would be peaceful and un-interfered with. At the stroke of midnight, the celebrating participants gathered all along the frontier fence would calmly take out their wire cutters and dismantle the fence. This will be under the cover of a huge fireworks display, with music, dancing and an overall fiesta image.

The successful and professional planning of the event was paramount, and it should be funded by the European Community and take place under the European Flag. That way both Spanish and British nationalism would be successfully removed from the event.

David Henley left the Jimena meeting and went up onto the roof of the Hostel Anon. It was good to be alone, to come to terms with this totally unexpected turn of events. He took a beer from the fridge and sat down. It was then that he noticed a familiar perfume; at first, he could not place it. He thought hard for a moment, it was the perfume used by Anna Marie Salsun. His eyes were becoming used to the dark and, as he stared into the darkness he could just make out the silhouette of a woman.

"Anna, is that you?"

There was no reply, and he realised that she was crying. He picked his way carefully around the tables and chairs and finally reached where she was sitting, right at the edge of the flat roof.

"I'm alright; I'm not going to throw myself off or anything stupid."

"What's the problem?" he asked.

"Oh, it's many problems, a mixture of sadness, anger, hope, and relief." He took a clean handkerchief from his pocket and passed it to her.

"You British are always so prepared for anything; do you always keep a clean hanky for the distressed woman?" She dried her eyes and sighed.

"My husband would have been so pleased to know what is planned tonight. I have tried to take his place, to take the actions he would approve of, but I am not him, I am not a man. I want to play my part and I am infuriated that women were excluded from tonight's deliberations. Everything about this movement is right but for the exclusion of women. But I suppose we have to take things one at a time. I am determined to one day become a member of the new Frontera Assembly, but that will be after many gender battles I know."

"Did you come alone?" asked David.

"No. I came with Bobby, but we had a row and he's left without me. He is such a chauvinist; it must be the trickle-down effect of working for the Prince. They only have one use for women."

"Why don't we have a drink and I'll drop you back to Soto."

By now he could see quite clearly, he moved across to the bar, poured a generous measure of Ballentine's into a tumbler and added a little water.

"Here, this should do the trick."

"You are so comforting, David, Rosemary is a lucky woman."

"I am not always so perfect you know. We all have our good times and bad times."

Chapter 14

"Albert, you look fed up, more problems at work?" Carmen Stagnetto was busying herself in the kitchen, the aroma of chicken stock and thyme signalled her special risotto was on the way. But not for Albert; he would have protein and cabbage with a little parmesan cheese and watch with envy as his wife and daughter enjoyed the high 'carbo' fix!

Everything to do with food made Albert Stagnetto feel content, especially rice, pasta and bread. Now he was not allowed any of his favourite food. Fifteen years or so ago, it was sex that drove him on, but things had changed both for him and Carmen. It was still good but infrequent, and their relationship had lost its zing. Oh well, that's life, and in today's world, it's only youngsters who have sex!

"That smells great Carmen, but I can't sit and watch you eat it. I'll take my cold chicken and eat it in front of the TV. I am really fed up with this bloody diet." With that, he made his way to the sitting room and the prospect of some brain-numbing drama. The Six O'clock news was on Gib TV and their political reporter, who also wrote in the Gibraltar Chronicle, was spouting off about the rumours of a conspiracy, saying that he could not find a minister or person in authority on either side of the frontier who wanted to be interviewed on the subject. A cloak of silence had dropped very effectively on the whole matter.

The phone rang and Albert jumped up with a start. It was the governor's office; the governor wanted to see Albert immediately; some dramatic information had just come to hand. Chewing hard on the last piece of cold chicken, Albert rushed into the kitchen where Carmen and Antonia... were just starting on the delicious risotto. He told them he had been summoned to Government House, said he didn't know what time he'd be back, grabbed his jacket and ran down the stairs and into Main Street.

Chapter 15

David Henley looked to where the voice came from. "Vladimir Kurshon, at your service." The owner of the voice was like something out of a poor 'B' movie. Smoking a Russian cigarette, swarthy unshaven look, bulging jacket. "Hello," said David. "Interesting information; is it true?"

He beckoned me to join him at his table. Only resident in Spain for the past four months; former media boss in Moscow, he looked uncomfortable – may be looking for a 'reason d'etre.'

He told me that the events of 9/11 had seriously damaged his 'business.' When TV was released from state control in Russia, he became the controlling shareholder in the former Soviet Union's second-largest TV network. But things had not worked out and he was held responsible for a massive loss. In fact, the funding package had been backed by a branch of the Moscow mafia. They eventually made him an offer he couldn't refuse: take the large pot of cash illegally raised on the very new Moscow stock market to Spain and invest it in the property. Buy houses in Sotogrande, move your family and settle in Spain. Look after the investments well, and you will be secure for life. Refuse and we can't guarantee how long that life will be! So here he was, living in a huge house, with servants, bodyguards, a yacht, several Mercs, and bored to death. The burnt-out boat was one of a dozen he owned, he had arranged for it to be brought from the Gulf to the boat yard in Soto for repairs, but when the inside had been stripped out, the gold bullion was missing. Vladimir told me that the remaining 11 craft were being brought to Spain and that he hoped the treasure stored in the bilges would be intact. He said he knew about the aborted plans for the joining of Gibraltar to Andalusia; was not surprised that the Sultan of Borogi had reneged on the deal. He then said that the bullion on its way to Soto would certainly be enough to replace the lost Borogi funding. He would be prepared to support the cause if there was a place for him in the new Government.

Chapter 16

In August 2002 the remaining Autovia between Estapona and Torreguadiaro was opened along with the redoubled coast road, suddenly life was easier! The problems between Cadiz and Malaga provinces had been settled over road funding.

Gibraltar was in a state of fury; the Blair Government negotiating with Madrid, over the heads of the people of Gibraltar. It seemed impossible that neither Government had picked up on the dissension in Andalusia, the three-year-old plan for the province to cede from Spain and unite with Gibraltar. The withdrawal of Borogi funds had fixed the plan as a frozen secret.

"I want to meet the Gomez brothers soon before it's too late. Once Gibraltar holds its referendum it will be too late to move." Vladimir seemed very well briefed for an outsider who had only been in Spain for less than six months. I asked him how he had such good intelligence. His reply was stark and to the point; money – cash especially – encourages lax behaviour. There was lots of cash, therefore lots of secrets for sale.

I had to talk to Anna Marie, she was the best point of contact with the Gomez cousins who had been paying me but not talking to me since the plan lost its initial funding.

Chapter 17

Albert was in a reflective mood, thinking about the frantic phone call from the governor's office three years previously, an episode which had ended with police raids on both sides of the frontier and the smashing of a Russian drugs plot that had attempted to use the so-called Andalusia-Gibraltar conspiracy for independence as a cover for a massive import of hard drugs into Europe.

Twenty Russians, plus Spanish and Gibraltarian nationals including the Gomez cousins and several mayors from the 'Frontera' towns had been arrested and tried; all but one of the mayors had received jail terms of ten years. Anna Marie Salsun had been cleared of all charges against her but had returned to Argentina; she was no longer popular with the authorities in southern Spain and on the Rock.

Things for Albert Stagnetto had, however, improved; with the Gomez cousins in prison, Jose in Madrid and Phillipo in the UK at Wandsworth, there were no longer powerful politicos standing between him and promotion. The governor had recommended Inspector Stagnetto for promotion and an honour, likely to be an MBE, for his part in smashing the conspiracy. The long overdue promotion to Chief Inspector had come a year earlier and this new status had done wonders for his self-confidence and his bank balance. He also had the use of a driver and car for official business. It had transported him to the regular monthly meeting across the frontier in San Roque with his brother-in-law; a semi-official gathering to help combat the growing threat of terrorism, increased drug smuggling and money laundering by organised gangs from Africa and the former Eastern block The Rock's close proximity to the world just across the Straits of Gibraltar had changed policing and security methods forever. And, life at home was much improved between him and his wife and, surprisingly, between him and his daughter. Not all was well, she was still out late at night; not telling them where she was going and who she was with, but she was much more outwardly thoughtful and friendly; a compromise, but a worthwhile compromise.

He had given up on the Atkins diet but so far had not regained any weight; he was just controlling his food intake, not overdoing the rice and pasta!

Work-wise his seniority had made a huge difference to his world of work. He organised and apportioned all the detective work, liaised with the governor's office, was responsible for relations with the Royal Military Police, and had a watching brief over the uniformed PCs at the frontier with Spain. His close relationship with his Spanish counterparts in La Linea and San Roque was viewed as an asset, not a hindrance as in the past when Phillipo Gomez never gave up trying to ruin his career with sideways hints of overt familiarity with his Spanish brother-in-law.

Something, however, was puzzling Chief Inspector Stagnetto on this hot and humid afternoon; the imminent return of David Henley to the Rock in an official capacity.

Henley had silently vanished from the Campo de Gibraltar just prior to the smashing of the conspiracy; just vanished into the night. All attempts to contact him via the foreign office in London were rebuffed in a cool and superior fashion. Now, some four years after the event, the governor's office had announced that DH (as he was now referred to) was returning as a special advisor to the governor on defence and security matters and would be the senior official liaising with Gibraltar Government and Britain's EC partner Spain; a big job indeed!

Britain's role in Europe was not easy. The UK Independence Party, having scored a major battle in the European elections, was pushing for the UK to leave the European Union completely. David Cameron's government was increasingly unpopular, having misread the runes completely in mistakenly agreeing to a referendum on the matter.

Gibraltar's position was confused; it had always flown the EC flag and had ambitions to be an independent territory within the Union. What if the UK was to withdraw; where would that leave the Rock; its closest EC contact and neighbour would be Spain, Gib's oldest foe! Maybe the proposed link between the Rock and Andalusia could be reborn; there had to be some way of ensuring Gib's future in the extended EU.

Chapter 18

Somewhere a phone was ringing; in his dream, Albert Stagnetto was shouting at his daughter to answer it. He awoke with a start, realising it was his mobile. What time was it, not yet dawn; still dark and unbearably hot and humid – he hated this time of year. Where the hell had he left the mobile; it had stopped ringing now and he was tempted to go back to bed. Something told him that the call was important; they usually rang him on the landline if it was regular police night business. He couldn't find the bloody thing; he picked up the landline phone and punched in his mobile's number. The ringtone led him downstairs to the fridge; the mobile was just about to vibrate itself off the top. Grabbing at it, he missed and it sailed across the kitchen, landing with a thud under the table where the battery disconnected itself from the body of the phone. Shit, things were never easy when he was awoken from a deep and distressing dream.

He re-attached the battery and switched the mobile on again. In a few seconds, he was looking at the missed calls menu; the most recent of which was his own landline number. Scrolling down he read out the second number; it was Sergeant Olivier's! He pressed the call button and waited.

"Hello, sir, I'm so glad I got you; your landline is answering unobtainable right now, have you forgotten to pay the bill?"

"Of course not; you're fired! Now come to the point, why wake me in the middle of the night."

"The RAF/MOD police have picked up the body of an Englishman at the Algeciras Bay end of the runway, it's in a pretty mangled state but they think they've identified it; a David Henley of the FCO, the diplomat who was to help solve all out problems with Spain."

"I'll be right over, what about formal identification?" The line went dead; his battery had died.

Albert struggled into his clothes, it was too early to shave and no time for a cool shower. Whilst there had been rumours that David Henley had already arrived on Gib, there had been no sightings either official or unofficial. Albert thought that Henley would have flown in from Gatwick, but that was just a gut feeling. He could have come in via Malaga or even Seville but this seemed unlikely as the FCO was paying his fare. On his way to Police HQ, he 'phoned the duty officer at the airport and asked whether they had any record of someone arriving on a British diplomatic passport during the past few days. As it was the middle of the night, this exercise would take a little time.

Sergeant Olivier was waiting at the front entrance to the HQ, he looked genuinely worried. "Hi Boss, this is a bad do if it really is David Henley; we're hoping for a positive ID, within the next hour or so, Henley's brother just happens to live on a converted finca near Jimena de la Frontera; he's on his way now."

Albert Stagnetto frowned and scratched his forehead; he was still full of sleep and finding it difficult to think straight.

"What do we know so far, not even how long the body's been in the sea; is there any visible evidence of an attack or did he just slip and fall? Anyhow, we must wait for a positive ID before speculating I suppose?"

Olivier looked quizzically at his boss who seemed unnaturally fazed by what was developing. Stagnetto looked at him. "When will his brother get here; shouldn't be too long at this time of night. The frontier is quiet too, can you check with our boys down there?"

At that moment Olivier's mobile rang. "Yes, why would they do that? What, they've arrested him; on what charge?" He motioned to his boss. "Henley's brother has just been arrested by the goons on the other side." The sergeant's loathing of the Spanish knew no bounds.

"I'll have a word with my brother-in-law at San Roque tomorrow, I guess we'll just have to wait for a formal ID?"

The sergeant drove down Main Street and dropped his boss outside Carlos Brothers. Main Street had been pedestrianised two years previously and even the police were forbidden to drive along it unless on an emergency call, blue lights flashing, but at 4.30 am the rules did not apply to Sergeant Olivier. Albert crept up the stairs, undressed silently and crawled back into bed, trying not to disturb Carmen, but she was already awake.

"I thought they would keep you longer, what's going on?" Her tone was definitely one of displeasure at having her sleep interrupted.

He told her about the body and how, at a guess, it was David Henley and that confirmation had been delayed due to Colin Henley being arrested by the Policia Local on the Spanish side. He would phone his brother-in-law Ramon in

San Roque first thing in the morning to find out what the hell was going on. With that said he dropped into a deep, dreamless sleep.

Chapter 19

Antonia Stagnetto woke suddenly, where was she; it was pitch dark and her head was throbbing. She tried to move her arms but her wrists felt numb and immovable. What the hell was going on? She tried to sit up but that was impossible with her hands tied behind her back. She tried to remember her last movements; they had ended up at the K Bar in the port at Sotogrande having had a long indulgent evening in a bar at Puerto Banus. She had consumed a fair amount of alcohol, but nothing out of the ordinary, and shared a joint or two with friends, but she should not be feeling like this. And how had she got here; where was here? She tried to concentrate but it would not come. She slumped back into a half sleep half stupor in which she noticed the drink in her hand gave off a strange aroma; had the drink tasted odd, was it her imagination? Then she was rowing in a skiff and her right hip was hurting. Rowing, hip-hurting Rohypnol – no it could be; had she been date-raped? She awoke again with a jolt; a bright light was shining in her eyes; her head still hurt like hell. She felt so cold and then realised that her clothes had been removed.

"Señorita Stagnetto, are you alright, it is you?" The young constable sounded anxious as he removed his jacket and placed it over Antonia's nude form. "I must call your father, what will he make of all this."

"Where am I, what has happened to me?" She started to sob.

"You're safe now; we found you here in response to an anonymous phone call. How you got here is a mystery, this guard hut has not been used since the frontier re-opened some 20 years ago." The PC spoke into his personal radio, "Please get an ambulance to the eastern end of the runway as soon as possible, and inform the Chief Inspector that we have his daughter in our care; she is in shock and appears to be suffering from the after-effects of a drug overdose. Also, have a female doctor on standby; I think she may have been sexually assaulted." His last words were spoken softly so that she would not hear.

"Albert, wake up," Carmen Stagnetto was shaking him so hard; she was crying and her voice was shrill. He recognised the shrillness; a shrillness that only occurred when Carmen was desperate. "It's Antonia, something awful has happened to her. Sergeant Olivier is downstairs with a car, we're going to the airstrip; do hurry up." For the second time that night, he had been woken from a deep sleep; this time he was visibly shaking and his heart was racing. Telling himself to calm down he tried to concentrate on what Sergeant Olivier was saying. "She's safe, sir, but in a poor state. Young PC Immaculata is with her, so she's in safe hands." What a name for a policeman, if it was his he'd have changed it at the first opportunity.